MYSTERIES I

MISSING GEMS OF THE TAJ MAHAL

Lyndon C.

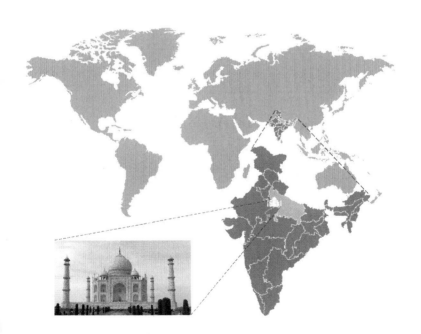

Interior illustrations by Ananya Chopra

ISBN: 1546381139
ISBN-13: 978-1546381136

To my wife Mugdha, without whom this would have remained an idea in my head. I couldn't build you the Taj Mahal; I hope this dedication will suffice.

To my two voracious readers Roshan and Kovid, for their brutally honest feedback. I'm glad you did not outgrow this book by the time I finished writing it.

Special thanks to our family friend and budding fifth grade artist, Ananya Chopra, for bringing Sid's journey to life through her hand-drawn illustrations.

Table of Contents

CHAPTER ONE
Cc-rrr-u-nnn-ccc-hhh

Sid was squinting at his camera's screen in the bright sunlight, trying to take a picture of the construction site in front of him. He was in a strange land, at a strange time, with thousands of laborers nearby building a gigantic white monument. He was startled by a loud thump behind him; he turned around to see an approaching elephant. He jumped out of the way in time, but the camera slipped out of his hand.

He covered his eyes as the elephant lumbered past him and stepped on the camera.

"Cc-rrr-u-nnn-ccc-hhh". Sid had a sickening feeling in his stomach as he peeked through his fingers. His camera lay crushed on the ground a few steps away. The elephant continued up a dusty ramp, straining to pull a cart with a large block of white marble. No one had noticed what happened, not one of the thousands of laborers busy working around him. The elephant was one of many others slowly pulling loads of white marble up the ramp to the base of a structure that was the hub of all the activity. The structure resembled the majestic Taj Mahal in India, except that Sid was witnessing it being built!

Sid carefully picked up the damaged camera and shook the loose pieces of glass from the cracked display. 'I've owned this camera for just over a year and I've already damaged it,' thought Sid. 'What will Dad and Mom say about it?' Last year, when his parents had noticed that Sid was getting good at composing pictures with his dad's camera, they had surprised him with his own camera and a photography class on his tenth birthday. Sid loved the camera - it was a nice compact camera - small enough to slide into his pocket, yet with a powerful zoom to get close up pictures.

He looked around. He felt trapped in a history book, one of the many he had been reading as he prepared for his school district's history bowl. He heard some more thumping and jumped back and fell. And he kept falling...

CHAPTER TWO
Jet Lag

Sid woke up with a jolt! He looked around sleepily – his dad was gently snoring in the unfamiliar bed to his left. That was all just a vivid dream. The clock on the nightstand between them glowed 3:30 AM. The glow was bright enough for him to make out a word on the pen in front of the clock: 'Agra'.

It slowly came back to him – the bed and room were unfamiliar because he was in a hotel in Agra in north India.

They had arrived late last night after a long car ride from the airport in New Delhi, the capital of India. He didn't remember much of the car ride after getting in the back seat. He was drowsy and there wasn't much to see out of the window that time of night. The soft drone of music in a strange language on the car radio had slowly lulled him to sleep.

His dad had warned him about jet lag when they were back home in America planning their trip. He had laughed when his dad explained that since they were crossing over 10 time zones in a day, their bodies would get confused and not know when to sleep or be awake.

"Yay! I can watch TV in the middle of the night!" he had exclaimed to his dad.

"It also means you may nod off when you are doing something interesting in the middle of the day", his dad had reminded him in a calm tone.

But as he lay awake in bed, TV was the last thing on his mind. He wondered how Luke and Joseph, his best friends in elementary school, were spending their winter break.

Sid was a history buff and had formed his school's team for the National History Bowl. He had a lot of bookish knowledge of history, but had always dreamed of visiting historic landmarks around the world. When he found out that his dad had to travel to Agra for business, he had begged his dad to take the family along, since this would be a great opportunity to visit one of the wonders of the modern world - the Taj Mahal!

His parents had discussed it at length since they wouldn't all be able to go on this trip together as a family. His sister had to travel for a sports tournament during those dates. Sid could either attend the tournament with them or accompany his dad. When his parents presented him with the choice, he chose Agra without a second thought.

He was so excited, that he had started preparing for the trip immediately. He went to the library and looked up travel guides to India. One was a comprehensive, but heavy, 1,200-page book about the whole country - too big! There were some specifically about the big cities in India like Delhi and Mumbai; others about popular tourist destinations like the beaches of Goa and the backwaters of Kerala. He finally found a guidebook about Agra and two other nearby cities and skimmed through the pages.

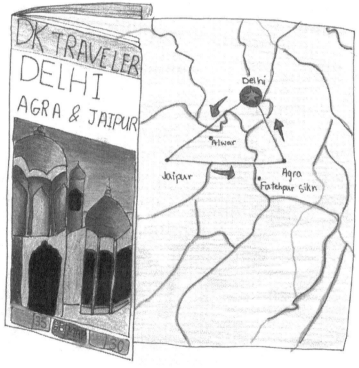

The guidebook covered the three most visited cities in India's northwest region - Delhi, Agra and Jaipur. Delhi is the capital of

India, Agra is home to the Taj Mahal, while Jaipur is known as the pink city because of its pink structures. These three cities form what is referred to as the "golden triangle" because of their richness in culture and history, and on a map, they lie at the three corners of a triangle.

Sid liked that the guidebook was not big and bulky, and the section dedicated to Agra was substantial. It had glossy pages, plenty of photographs and illustrations of the Taj Mahal and described its history and architecture in great detail.

He wrote down the name of the guide and asked his dad to use his allowance to buy him the most recent edition.

He had read through the book a few times at home. During the long, 16-hour non-stop flight from New Jersey to New Delhi, he re-read parts and made a list of things he wanted to do and see in Agra.

Sid started feeling sleepy again, and less than a minute after shifting into his favorite sleeping position, he was fast asleep.

The clock on the nightstand read 3:59 a.m.

CHAPTER THREE
Money Matters

Sid woke up to the smell of breakfast. "Good morning sleepyhead! Looks like you slept better than I did," his dad said, "I've been awake since 4:30 am. I gave up trying to sleep and caught up with my work."

"Actually Dad, I got my first taste of jet lag too" replied Sid, "I was awake between 3 and 4 a.m. this morning. What time is it now?"

"It's past 8 a.m. I was going to give you a

few more minutes before waking you up to reduce some of that jet lag" his dad admitted. "I was hoping the smell of your favorite breakfast would wake you up."

"Sunny side up eggs and toast. Thanks, Dad!"

As Sid ate his breakfast, his dad discussed his work schedule for the next few days. His meetings would keep him busy until late afternoon, but he would be free in the evenings, as well as on the last day.

"Sorry Sid, they moved these meetings so we could have the last day off. But Mr. Verma from the Agra office offered to have his son accompany you while I'm at work. He's about your age and should be great company."

"It's OK Dad," replied Sid. "At least we have a full day to ourselves. The guidebook said that the attractions in Agra are open until sunset. That will give us an hour or two for sightseeing together. But tell me more about Mr. Verma's son. What's his name? What do you know about him?"

"His name is Raj, and he too is on winter break. From Mr. Verma's description, you two will have a lot in common. He is a history buff too."

Sid was excited and a bit nervous at the same time. He was looking forward to making a new friend, but wondered how they would get along. Would they really have a lot in common? He hoped Raj could speak English. The guidebook mentioned that India had over 100 major languages, three of which were commonly spoken by people in the area they were visiting.

Sid brushed those thoughts away. "Raj... that rhymes with Taj!" he chuckled. "The guidebook lists so many must-see places in and around Agra. I hope he can help me decide."

"I'm sure he knows the must-see sights for visitors like us" his dad replied. "I have a feeling that he may be able to give you a lot more information about the area and the attractions than your guidebook."

"Wait - if you are going to work, how will we travel to the must-see sights?" asked Sid.

"The two of you can use the chauffeured car while I carpool with Raj's dad. I'm counting on you to tell me which landmark we should visit on my day off, though something tells me that it will be the Taj Mahal!"

"I think so too, Dad. I was reading up about the Taj Mahal on the flight here and found it fascinating. I had only heard it called 'one of the most beautiful monuments in the world', but it actually is a tomb, or to use a new word I learned - 'mausoleum'. The guidebook had so many details that I keep referring back to it – I'm carrying it with me everywhere on this trip."

"That's a great idea, Sid. Make sure your camera memory card has enough free space and your batteries are charged. Which reminds me, I need to give you some money since I won't be with you today," his dad said, opening his wallet. The bills were of different shapes, sizes, and colors. He took out a few bills, counting them out five bills of 500, and five bills of 100.

Sid's eyes grew wide in amazement. "Three thousand! That's a lot of money, isn't it? Is it all real? Why are you giving me so much?

His dad smiled, "These are Indian rupee notes, the currency used here, just like we use dollars in America..."

"How come they all look different?" he interrupted his dad, "Why don't we use our own money here?"

"Unlike our bills which are all similar in shape, size and color, Indian notes are different for different denominations. Every country has its own money, and the value of each country's currency is different too. In this case, three thousand rupees is the equivalent of about fifty U.S. dollars."

"Oh! It seemed like a lot, but after converting it to dollars, it is manageable - I can handle that! That's about how much sis and I spend at the movie theater."

"I'm sure you will be able to manage. The hotel staff told me that it should be more than enough for entrance fees, food for the two of you, and for some souvenirs."

"Should I ask Raj if I'm not sure about the cost of something?" asked Sid.

"That's a good idea - he should be able to help."

Sid was finishing the last of his breakfast. "When will I get to meet Raj?"

"We will be meeting Raj and his dad in our hotel lobby in 30 minutes, so get ready."

CHAPTER FOUR
New Friend

A few minutes before 9:30 a.m., Sid and his dad headed down to the hotel lobby. People often told Sid how much he resembled his dad. Like his dad, he was tall and lean, and had very similar facial features. He also inherited a few habits from his dad, like double-checking everything.

He checked his black drawstring bag again in the elevator. Travel guide, pencil, water bottle, snack bars and his camera - he had not forgotten anything. As his dad had suggested, he had distributed the money in different pockets for safety.

When they reached the lobby, his dad scanned the area for his colleague. He didn't see any familiar faces, so he picked a spot with a clear view of the hotel entrance. As soon as they sat on the over-sized chairs, Sid pulled out his guidebook and spread out a map of the area.

"Sid, if you keep studying that guidebook, you'll be my expert on the area. Remember to think about what we should do together after I get back from work this evening." His dad looked toward the hotel entrance and stood up, "I think that may be them!"

Sid closed his guidebook and looked up. He saw a father and son duo walking hurriedly toward them. The boy was wearing a bright blue t-shirt, jeans, and gray sneakers. His hair was neatly combed and he wore glasses.

'He looks normal,' Sid thought.

"Good morning Mr. Cooper," said Mr. Verma, sticking out his hand. "It's nice to finally meet you in person after all those online Skype meetings. Please accept my sincerest apologies for being late. We were stuck in traffic. But don't worry; if we leave soon, we should still be able to reach office in time for our first meeting." He shifted his gaze to Sid, "Wait, where are my manners? This strapping young boy must be Sid!"

He turned to his son and said, "This is my son Raj. *Beta*, say *namaste* to Uncle and Sid."

"Good morning Uncle!" Raj said. Turning toward Sid, he smiled and said, "Hi, I'm Raj, and I'm in the 5th standard. What standard are you in?"

Sid was relieved that Raj spoke English. 'What does he mean by standard?' he wondered.

"He means what grade, *beta,*" Raj's dad clarified, as if he read Sid's mind. "We call it 'standard' in India."

"Oh - I'm in 5th grade too. I was so happy when my dad said I would have someone my own age to spend the day with. I hope I didn't ruin any plans you had." Sid smiled. "This is my first time in India, so I am glad I have someone from here who knows the area better than I do!"

"My pleasure," Raj replied. "I probably would have read a book at home or played a video game, nothing exciting. Did you have something you wanted to do today?" he asked, looking at the guidebook in Sid's hand.

"Could we start with the biggest landmark - the Taj Mahal?" Sid asked. I have been reading up on it and am fascinated by its history."

"Absolutely! I have been there about a dozen times with family and friends, but it always looks different depending on the time of day and the season. I've seen it orange, beige and many shades of white, and once could almost not see it because of the fog. I wonder what it will look like today."

The fathers were talking in whispers a few steps away.

"I think that amount of money should be more than enough," Sid overheard Mr. Verma say.

Turning to them he said, "Boys, it sounds like you are visiting the Taj Mahal today. We will be in meetings all day, but Raj knows how to contact me if you need anything. My driver will take you there. Let me give him a few instructions and then we can head to office while you two have fun!"

The doorman at the hotel asked them for the names of their drivers and announced them on a microphone. The announcement could be heard from speakers in the parking lot outside the hotel. Their drivers slowly pulled up their cars to the hotel entrance. Mr. Verma spoke to his driver in a local language. The only words Sid could understand was "Taj" and "parking".

Raj explained that his dad was talking to the driver in Hindi, one of the official languages of India. He asked the driver to drop them off at the Eastern gate entrance of the Taj and wait for them in the Taj parking lot. After they were done, he would take the two of them for lunch and any other sights but was to drop them back at the hotel before 4 p.m.

"Do you speak English and Hindi?" Sid asked.

"English, Hindi and a bit of Punjabi," replied Raj. "What about you?"

"English, but I know a few words in Spanish," Sid said.

Sid felt relieved that he had a translator in Raj. He felt silly for being a bit anxious earlier. 'I think we're going to get along well,' he thought as he got into the waiting car.

CHAPTER FIVE
An Accident

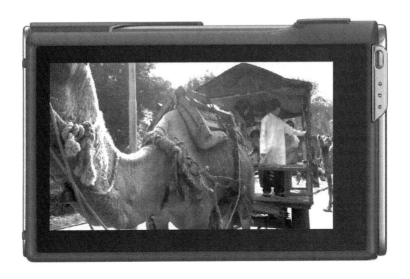

The ride was a short one. When they reached the parking lot, Sid looked around unsuccessfully for any sign of the Taj Mahal.

As if reading Sid's mind, Raj said, "If you are trying to catch a glimpse of the Taj, you won't be able to see it from here. The Taj was getting discolored and turning yellow because of pollution. To prevent additional damage, the government created a 500-meter zone around the Taj Mahal where vehicles that run on diesel, gasoline or petroleum are not allowed."

"Is the Taj permanently discolored?" asked Sid, remembering that the Taj was renowned for its white marble.

"No, it isn't. The government recently started a multi-year mud-pack treatment to get rid of the Taj's tan," said Raj.

"Mud-pack?" Sid asked in disbelief.

"Yes, I couldn't believe it either. It was in the news recently. They plaster a thin layer of lime-rich clay over the marble surface and leave it to dry overnight. They remove the dried mud with soft nylon brushes and wash it with distilled water," Raj explained. "This is considered safe since it has minimal chemicals and is done by hand."

"I learned something new today, thanks to you!" Sid exclaimed. He knew a lot about the Taj Mahal from the guidebook, but it was mostly general information. He knew that the monument was commissioned in 1632 by Mughal emperor, Shah Jahan, as a tomb for his favorite wife, Mumtaz Mahal. Apart from the tomb, the complex had a mosque, guest house, and gardens. It was designated as a UNESCO World Heritage Site in 1983, and is considered one of the wonders of the world.

"How far away did you say the Taj is from here?" Sid asked.

"500 meters," said Raj and he guided them to the ticket counter.

Sid mentally converted the 500-meter distance to approximately 1500 feet, a measure he was more familiar with. That wouldn't take long to walk.

"Do we have to walk from here?" asked Sid.

"We could either walk, or take an electrical vehicle to the entrance of the Taj," replied Raj. "Let's take the cart and save our energy for all the walking we will be doing inside the Taj complex - it is huge, you know."

"It is over 40 acres, according to my guidebook," said Sid, patting his travel guide.

Tickets in hand, they walked over to the waiting electrical golf cart. They were the last two to get in before it slowly made its way to the Taj. The ride was bumpy because of unevenly paved roads and potholes, but Sid held on to the safety bar on the cart. They passed groups of people also headed in the same direction - many walking, some on cycle rickshaws.

"Sid look ahead! There's a camel cart taking passengers to the Taj," Raj pointed out. Sid leaned out for a better look and counted 6, no, 7 people piled in the back of a tall cart being slowly pulled by a camel. As they overtook the cart, he quickly dug his camera out of his bag for a picture. He leaned out of the golf cart, trying to single-handedly take a picture. Just as he clicked the button, their cart bumped over another pothole. A few passengers in the golf cart gasped as they were thrown a few inches up in the air.

Sid scrambled to hold onto the safety bar. As he fumbled, the camera slipped out of his hand and fell on the road! "Stop!" Sid blurted out, "My camera fell down!"

"Roko!" Raj called out in Hindi to the driver to stop the cart.

The cart slowed down. Sid looked back and saw the camera just in front of the camel cart. Things seemed to move in slow motion as the metal-lined wheels of the cart went over the camera.

"Cc-rrr-u-nnn-ccc-hhh". The sound

reminded Sid of his dream the previous night when the elephant stepped on his camera. This was déjà vu, but this time it was for real! As was the sickening feeling in his stomach.

CHAPTER SIX
Taj Bazaar

The electric cart slowly came to a stop, as did the sole bicycle rickshaw behind it. Their driver got down and escorted Sid and Raj to the remains of the camera.

The camera was crushed, the glass from the lens cracked and spread out on the road, and the flash broken. Sid carefully picked up the damaged camera, shook the loose pieces of glass and put it in an empty Ziploc plastic bag.

He had owned the camera for a little over a year, but it had been a constant companion since he received it. Sid could not believe he had dropped his camera and it was now destroyed. Between his sister and him, he was the careful one, who always took good care of his belongings. Sid's sadness over his crushed camera was only eclipsed by his uneasiness about breaking the news to his dad.

The camel continued its slow gait, unaware of the damage it had caused.

"I'm sorry that your camera broke," Raj said apologetically. "I hope the memory card was not damaged, so you will at least have the pictures on it."

The driver walked them back to the electric cart, and they got back on. A few curious passengers asked Raj, in Hindi, what had happened and he explained that the camera was broken.

After a few sympathetic exchanges, Raj turned to Sid, who was sitting with his head hung low in sadness, "One passenger mentioned that there are a few shops around the Taj where you may be able to get another camera."

"Do you know where these shops are?" asked Sid feeling hopeful.

"I think so. The shops near the gates of the Taj are mainly souvenir shops targeting tourists. We're in luck today - there is a local street bazaar every Thursday, where people put out tables and sell new and old items. You may be able to buy a used camera there."

"That sounds like a flea market." If he could get an inexpensive replacement, Sid wouldn't have to ask his dad. He had a spending threshold below which he did not have to ask for permission. His voice turned to a whisper, "How much will it cost? My dad gave me some money that I can use, but I can only spend some of it without asking his permission, and I don't want to disturb him during his meetings."

"How much can you spend?" Raj asked.

Sid did some mental math, converting dollars to rupees. "Not more than 1500 rupees for a used camera", he said, thinking about the price tag of his now damaged camera, and his spending threshold. "It doesn't have to be fancy, as long as I can take some nice pictures today and the next few days."

"Taj gates!" the driver called out as the cart stopped near a huge reddish-brownish wall.

"These walls have a very unique color - what are they made of?" Sid asked Raj.

"The outer walls of the complex are made of red sandstone, similar to the forts built by kings hundreds of years ago," replied Raj. "The Taj is walled on three sides, but the river-facing side is open."

Looking around, Sid noticed souvenir shops lining both sides of the street, spilling onto the sidewalk. Shopkeepers started calling out to them to visit their stores. "Magnets! Key chains! Inlaid marble items - just like the Taj!" they shouted, trying to tempt tourists with their wares.

Raj ignored them and walked on a narrow street along the wall of the complex. Sid followed him, keeping pace. The street narrowed as they went further, and the souvenir shops were replaced by one and two storied brick buildings that were built wall-to-wall. The shops here were selling daily necessities like fruits, vegetables and food.

"We are on the outskirts of Taj Ganj" Raj explained, as they passed a couple of stray dogs lazily observing them. "This area used to be a bazaar, or marketplace when the Taj was built. It had merchants selling items from all around the world. As you can see, a lot has changed."

Sid saw what Raj meant - both sides of the lane were lined with a random mix of tiny storefronts and tinier residences. Some of the houses advertised rooms for short stays: "Hotel room near Taj Mahal". Power lines were dangerously strung overhead.

The narrow lane was made narrower by cycles on their stands, parked horse carriages, and occasionally by discarded furniture. Stray animals claimed any comfortable spots.

"Are we nearing the flea market?" Sid asked.

"There it is - just up ahead!" replied Raj.

CHAPTER SEVEN
Another Camera

Sid surveyed the scene a few feet ahead of him.

There were makeshift stalls with collapsible tables encroaching on both sides of the lane. The haphazard arrangement allowed no more than two people to squeeze through, side by side.

"These vendors sell anything and everything, so keep an eye out for a camera,"

Raj told him.

"You look at the stalls on the left and I'll take the right," Sid suggested.

They passed tables covered with colorful plastic toys, brightly colored clothes, and household items.

"Raj, look!" Sid tugged on Raj's t-shirt, as he pointed to a spot they had just passed. A brown cloth was laid out on the ground and had a random assortment of used electronic items and toys. He saw a CD player, MP3 player, radio, and a couple of hot wheel cars. In the middle of it all was an old camera.

The kind-looking old man sitting behind the spread noticed their interest.

"Chahiye kya?" he asked in Hindi, before

switching to broken English. "You want? I give you good price." He slowly pieced the words together. "All working just fine. Music player or camera?" he asked, holding them out toward Sid.

Sid took the camera and turned it around in his hands. The make and model information had long faded and disappeared. The camera was bulky, like the first digital camera his dad had owned when Sid was growing up.

Sid found the power button and turned it on. The lens extended slowly, making a squeaking noise. The tiny screen on the back lit up. The settings dial had a few faded options. He turned the control to Auto Mode, pointed it at the street they had just come from and clicked. It made a loud 'click', and a picture of the horse carriage they had passed earlier appeared on the display.

"Works nice? I put new battery. For you, 1,500 rupees only," the old man offered. "This is special camera."

Raj turned to Sid and whispered, "If you want it, I can try bargaining to lower the price."

Sid whispered back, "It looks OK and

seems to work – I'll take it."

Raj whispered back, "Pretend not to be interested in it. Look at another stall, or start walking away."

Sid started looking at another table nearby.

Raj turned to the vendor, pointed to the camera and said, "1,500 rupees is too much for this old camera. We'll pay 750." After a few exchanges back and forth, they settled on ₹1,000.

Sid removed two ₹500 bills and handed them to the vendor.

"Shukriya - Thank-ooo!" the old man said, touching the money to his forehead. "May you have many interesting adventures with camera," he said with a twinkle in his eyes.

Sid wondered if there was a deeper meaning to what the mystic old man said, but didn't ponder over it as he explored the camera.

They traced their steps back to where the electric cart had dropped them off earlier.

"That was neat, getting me a deal on the camera!" Sid said. "Without you, I would have just paid him the asking price."

"We bargain all the time here," Raj replied. "It becomes second nature."

Sid was enjoying Raj's company, not just as a new friend, but as someone who was watching out for him.

They joined the security screening line to enter the Taj Mahal complex.

Sid noticed a group of monkeys on the metal roof above the metal detectors and snapped a few pictures as he waited. He captured shots of monkeys fighting over a fruit, security shooing away some monkeys, and two playful baby monkeys.

They finished their security screening a few minutes later and followed the path towards the main entrance.

CHAPTER EIGHT
A Teardrop

"That's the Great Gate," Raj pointed out to Sid, as they made their way through a growing crowd of people. The great gate had a tall central arch about two stories high. "It is supposed to mark a transition between the worldly market outside and a quiet paradise inside."

"The Taj Mahal! I see the Taj Mahal!" Sid exclaimed, pointing to a bright white dome that was visible above the inner walls of the complex. He pulled out his guidebook and flipped to the section about the Taj. The dome disappeared from view as they neared the great gate.

They entered the tall arch, surrounded by a crowd of visitors. About halfway in, Sid got his first full view of the Taj Mahal.

It was magnificent! Though he had seen many pictures of the Taj in the guidebook, none of them did the monument any justice. The monument looked like a white apparition rising in front of him, visible through the winter haze. It seemed to be floating above the heads of a sea of people, between the garden below and the sky above.

He wanted to capture this moment, so he held the camera as high as he could above the crowd of heads. He quickly took a picture of the arch framing the Taj Mahal.

After walking through the great gate, they landed on a platform. The platform stood high above the gardens, just like the Taj Mahal at the other end of the complex. People jostled their way to the front of the platform for a quick picture with the Taj in the background. Sid followed Raj and sat on a stone bench at the side, away from the crowds. A small tourist group was nearby, and they were listening intently to their local guide.

"If we eavesdrop, we will get a free introduction to the Taj!" Raj joked.

The guide started speaking to the group in a loud voice. "The Taj Mahal is one of the wonders of the world, built over 350 years ago by Mughal emperor Shah Jahan. He built it as a loving memorial for his third wife Mumtaz Mahal, who died during childbirth of their 14th child, leaving him heartbroken."

"14 children?" Sid chuckled. "My parents struggle with just the two of us!"

"Shah Jahan actually had sixteen children between all his wives, but only seven survived into adulthood," Raj informed him.

"They say it took 20,000 workers 22 years to build this complex," the guide droned on. "The marble, semi-precious stones, and other building materials were brought from all over the world to build this marvel. The cost at that time was estimated to be around 32 million rupees, which would be over 52 billion rupees in today's money. Follow me through the *charbaghs* as we go to take a closer look at the monument." He held up a brightly colored closed umbrella and the group followed him down the steps through the landscaped gardens.

"Whoa! That's around a billion American dollars!" exclaimed Sid. "Raj, is *'charbaghs'* an Indian word for gardens?"

"You're on the right track. *Bagh* is the Hindi word for garden, and *char* means four," Raj replied. "The guidebook may have a detailed description of it."

Sid opened the guidebook and scanned the page, "It says that it is a Persian style garden layout, where the garden is divided by walkways or flowing water into four smaller parts." He looked up and saw the central waterway with walkways on both sides dividing the garden into four quarters. Each of the quarters were in turn divided by paths into four gardens.

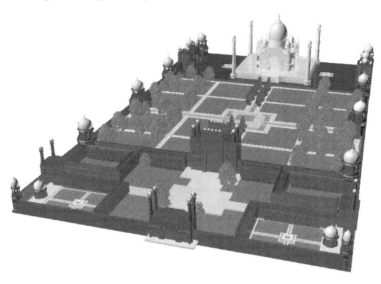

"Everything is so symmetrical here - the left and the right sides are perfect mirror images of each other!" Sid marveled.

The guidebook went on to describe how the gardens were very different from the original gardens almost four hundred years ago. Gardens of that era usually had fruit and flower bearing trees. However, in early 1900s, Lord Curzon, the British Viceroy in charge of India at that time, had the trees replaced with British-style grass lawns.

"Are you going to sit here and read all day?" asked Raj. "I thought you wanted to see the Taj Mahal, not read about it!"

"Thanks for reminding me. I often get carried away when reading," said Sid. As they walked down the walkway toward the Taj, he tried to picture what the original garden may have looked like. He imagined noblemen slowly strolling toward the Taj, stopping to pick an exotic fruit from a tree. Equally exotic and colorful birds probably flew between the trees and the water fountains.

"This is where we need to leave our shoes," said Raj, using his right foot to slip off his left shoe, and then the other way around. They were at base of the mausoleum.

Looking up, Sid realized that the Taj was not completely white as it had appeared from the great gate. Up close, he saw extensive colorful decorations and inscriptions on the face of the marble edifice.

Sid took off his shoes and left them in the shoe cubby. They climbed up a few stairs to what the guidebook, quoting famous Indian poet Rabindranath Tagore, had called "a teardrop on the cheek of time".

CHAPTER NINE
The Tomb

The steps led Sid and Raj to a large sandstone platform. The monument was in the center of the platform, built on a smaller, but taller marble platform. The tall white marble platform reflected the bright afternoon sun and stood in contrast to the surrounding red sandstone.

The first thing Sid noticed was the signature onion-shaped dome capping the monument. It was accentuated by four smaller domes at the four corners. The entire monument was built of white *Makrana* marble which appeared to change shades depending on the time of the day and sunlight.

The arches in the monument were surrounded by decorative colored floral designs and contrasting black patterns. As he looked around, he saw four tall towers at the four corners, which the guidebook called minarets.

Sid saw a long line of people snaking up to the marble steps that led up to the domed tomb. There had to be at least a few hundred people patiently waiting barefoot on the rough sandstone.

"It is going to take us a while to make it up there," Sid told Raj. The guidebook wasn't kidding when it said that over 3 million people visited the Taj each year.

"I'll bet your guidebook did not tell you how you can avoid this long line," teased Raj. "This long line is for local visitors from India, who pay a discounted entry fee. Do you see that other entrance over there without a line? That's the entrance for foreigners who paid higher entry fees. You are eligible to go through there and I will accompany you."

"You're a lifesaver!" Sid said as they walked up the other marble stairs. "If you hadn't told me, I would have been standing in that line forev—"

Sid left his sentence unfinished as he reached the top of the stairs. The majestic Taj loomed directly in front of him. Though there were hundreds of other tourists around, he was suddenly oblivious to everything else.

"Wow! This is amazing!"

As Sid walked toward the mausoleum, he referred to the two-page spread in his guidebook that identified elements of the main tomb in front of him. He realized that the black patterns were not designs, but beautiful Arabic calligraphy of verses from the Koran, the holy book of Islam. Looking closely, he realized that the calligraphy grew in size as it went higher, creating an optical illusion of a uniform script. That was no small feat for the Taj, which was as tall as a 20-story building.

The floral designs were not painted but were delicately cut and fitted precious stones inlaid in the marble surface, a technique the book called *pietra dura* in Italian or *parchin kari* in Hindi. Some of the flowers were so intricate that they had over 28 varieties of colored precious and semi-precious stones to create shaded effects.

The lower portions of the monument had decorative panels of flowers and plants realistically carved in the marble walls. He took a few photographs of these different decorative elements.

Sid and Raj joined the crowd of people entering the tomb. A security guard asked him to put the camera away since photography was not allowed in the inside chamber. He complied and entered the tomb.

Sid's eyes took a few seconds to adjust from the bright sunlight outside to the darkness inside. Light and cool breeze filtered through the lattice walls, balconies, and the ceiling. In the center, he saw the tomb of Mumtaz Mahal, with a slightly bigger tomb, for Shah Jahan placed to its left, the only nonsymmetrical element he had seen at the Taj complex.

"Did you know that they are not really buried in those tombs?" asked Raj. "These are actually empty tombs called cenotaphs. Their actual graves are at a lower level directly below them."

They walked around the octagonal marble screen surrounding the cenotaphs. They saw tour guides focus tiny flashlights behind the marble. The light shone through the translucent marble, making the flowers glow from within. They had to jostle through the incoming crowd to step back into the bright sunlight.

"This changes how I will look at tombs in cemeteries forever," Sid told Raj.

They walked on the warm marble floor toward a minaret in one corner of the platform overlooking the Yamuna River.

"Can I take a picture of the two of us with the Taj in the background?" Sid asked, pulling out his camera.

"Sure! Make sure you email it to me," replied Raj, straightening his hair.

"I wonder what it must have been like when they were building the Taj centuries ago," Sid said, turning on the camera. He looked for a timer option so he could take a delayed picture. He turned the camera dial to a faded option that resembled a clock - something his broken camera did not have. He pressed the button, stretched out his hand with the lens facing them and waited for the shutter to click.

The camera made a high-pitched whirring sound, followed by a bright flash of light that momentarily blinded them.

CHAPTER TEN
Way Back

Sid blinked a few times, trying to get his vision back. He could see bright spots dancing in front of his eyes, but they reduced with each blink. After a few seconds, he saw a blurry Raj, also blinking.

"That was a super bright flash! I can't wait to see the expressions on our faces in that picture," joked Raj. His gaze suddenly froze. "Wait, what happened to your clothes? How did you end up wearing a *kurta-pajama?*"

Sid looked at his own outfit, then at Raj's. His vision was back to normal. They were both dressed in similar clothes: thin loose fining cotton pants, with quarter button shirts that went down to their knees. Their shoes were cloth loafers with pointy toes!

The marble platform under his feet felt different. It didn't feel as smooth anymore.

Clink! Clank! Sid became aware of a continuous rhythmic tapping sound. He turned around, and could not recognize the tomb he had exited a few minutes ago. The magnificent Taj Mahal he had admired a few minutes ago was only half constructed! It was also partially covered in scaffolding. Sid looked around slowly. People were standing on the scaffolding, working on the edifice. Looking at the big arch over the entrance, he saw two stone cutters carving the flowing script. Small teams of other workers were smoothening the inlaid flower design patterns by rubbing it with grass. Dozens of laborers were squatting, chiseling and carving the marble base of the Taj.

"What just happened?" Raj asked, dazed.
"I was taking a picture of us in front of the

Taj," said Sid.

"When you were setting up the camera, you said, 'I wonder what it must have been like when they were building the Taj centuries ago'," Raj recalled.

"I did say that while I changed the setting to what looked like a worn out timer option on the camera," said Sid, looking closely at the camera dial.

"The camera flash was so bright that it temporarily blinded me," said Raj. "When I could see again, everything around us had changed. Including our clothes."

"Our clothes are similar to what these people are wearing. There are so many of them working here. And the Taj is still under construction," said Sid.

"If they're still building, that means—" Raj began slowly.

"—that means we traveled back in time!" Sid blurted.

"We traveled back over 350 years!!" exclaimed Raj. "How did this happen?"

"Do you remember how the old man who sold me the camera wished me 'interesting adventures' with the camera?" asked Sid. "He had a mysterious look in his eyes when he said that. Do you think there's something magical about this camera?"

"I had a funny feeling when I heard him say that," replied Raj, sounding concerned. "I hope the camera has a way to take us back!"

"I won't change the camera settings," Sid said, gingerly putting the camera away in his bag.

Sid surveyed the surrounding area. He realized that the entire complex was crawling with thousands of men, women and children, working on the other buildings and the fountains. He saw animals like elephants and buffaloes at work, pulling unused blocks of marble away from the site.

Looking in the other direction, he saw people working in the *charbaghs*. Though the gardens were not complete, they looked very different from what he saw earlier. He could now visualize what the guidebook had described. Laborers were busy transplanting fruit and flower bearing trees.

Sid found the unintentional history

lesson fascinating. "We are a part of history!" he exclaimed. "We cannot leave without exploring a little!"

"OK. But only for a few minutes," said Raj, caving in.

"Sounds like a plan!" said Sid, unable to hide his excitement.

"I didn't know they had mango, lemon and pomegranate trees in the gardens," marveled Raj.

As they walked through the gardens, they noticed a boy their age, helping his mother water the plants. He followed her, filling two buckets with water from the water pools, and watering the plants. He took a breather as they passed him and smiled at them.

"Mera naam Ramu hai," he introduced himself in Hindi as he waved to them. They smiled and waved back.

"Mera naam Raj, aur yeh hai Sid," said Raj introducing themselves in return. He continued talking to him in Hindi before turning to Sid.

"He's Ramu, and he works here alongside his parents, helping them earn money," Raj explained. "He asked if we were playing truant from school to see the emperor."

Sid was perplexed, "Huh? Emperor?"

Just then, they heard the foremen shouting. Workers started scrambling. Ramu spoke hurriedly with Raj, waved, and started sweeping the walkway.

"Ramu said that Emperor Shah Jahan was coming by boat to the site to monitor progress, and he had to get back to work," explained Raj.

"Do you think we can get a closer look at the emperor?" asked Sid.

The air filled with trumpet blasts and loud drum rolls.

CHAPTER ELEVEN
Missing Gems

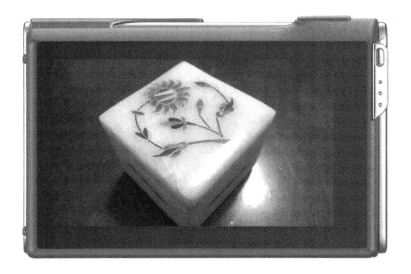

The trumpets and drums fell silent. The laborers stopped talking but continued working.

Sid and Raj had reached a quiet corner of the tomb's platform, where they could see the Yamuna River. There were a dozen regally decorated row boats docked on the river bank. A procession of well-dressed people was slowly making its way toward the monument. They were dressed in flowing robes, and their heads were covered with turbans of different shapes and colors.

"I think that's Emperor Shah Jahan," whispered Raj, pointing to a stately man in the middle of the procession. The emperor looked to be in his 60s and was flanked by guards. "He's the only one with a guard holding an umbrella over him, and another cooling him with a handheld fan made of peacock feathers."

"He's also the only one with feathers and jewels in his turban," observed Sid. "And he certainly is wearing the most jewelry and rings."

The royal procession climbed the stairs to the top of the marble platform. The supervising architect bowed down to greet the emperor. After a few exchanges, he walked alongside the emperor, showing him different areas of the monument. The emperor seemed pleased with the progress.

The emperor pointed at the flowers on the marble wall and spoke with the architect, but Sid could not understand the conversation. He looked questioningly at Raj.

"They're speaking in Hindi," Raj explained, "The emperor told Puruji that he is pleased with the flower inlays and carvings. He said they realize his dream of creating an eternal garden in paradise, making it a fitting resting place for Queen Mumtaz. He just summoned Chiranji, the chief sculptor and mosaicist."

The architect's assistant hurried toward a makeshift tent. He emerged with an older man, and they walked towards the emperor. Chiranji bowed down before the emperor.

As they were speaking, Raj translated the emperor's conversation. "I am very pleased with the workmanship of your people working on the inlays. Your team's work is exquisite. These delicate flowers will bloom forever."

Chiranji extended his worn hands and offered the emperor a small box. It was made of marble and was inlaid with precious stones, forming floral patterns similar to the ones on the walls of the Taj. The emperor accepted it, admired the work, and spoke again.

"This is a beautiful gift!" translated Raj, "Is there anything you need?"

Chiranji hesitated. The supervising architect seemed to reassure him. Chiranji spoke slowly in an apologetic tone, his eyes lowered.

"The chief mosaicist said that a few semi-precious stones intended for the inlay work have gone missing in the past two days. He trusts his workers and has absolutely no idea what happened to them. It will take months to find, and to transport replacement stones." Raj explained.

"What does he mean 'missing'? Are they misplaced or stolen?" asked Sid.

The emperor beckoned one of his accompanying courtiers. They had a whispered conversation before the advisor made an announcement: "The great emperor Shah Jahan is offering a reward for the return of the missing precious stones. The finder will be rewarded with a year's worth of wages."

"Ooh, we have a mystery to solve!" Sid whispered excitedly. "Raj, let's go find the missing jewels!"

CHAPTER TWELVE
Culprit Identified

"Where do we begin?" wondered Raj.

' "My favorite detectives always start by studying the crime scene," Sid replied. "Didn't they say that the jewels went missing from that tent over there?"

They took a closer look at the tent, which provided shade to the inlay artists. It shielded them from the glare of the bright sunlight as they turned odd shaped jewels into delicate carvings. The tent was a simple rectangular structure, made by tying faded bed sheets between four big bamboo sticks. The sheets covered three sides, and nearby trees provided them with shade from above.

Inside the tent, two men sat hunched over grinding stones. They were focused on cutting brightly colored stones into very thin sheets. Those thin sheets were then carefully carved into tiny shapes of flowers and leaves. These delicate and colorful carvings would be set in the marble walls of the Taj.

"There's only one way to get in or out," observed Raj. "It would be difficult for someone else to enter and steal those stones without being noticed."

Sid agreed. "The great detectives usually focus next on witnesses and suspects. But it looks like we don't have any witnesses."

"Should we involve Ramu?" asked Raj.

They walked over to the garden where they first met Ramu. He was taking a break from work and was resting under the shade of a tree. They joined him.

"Ramu, would you like to solve the mystery of the missing gems?" Raj asked him, in Hindi.

"I would love to, but I can only join you during my breaks," he replied.

"We don't have any witnesses, and don't know where to start with suspects," said Sid. "Any ideas?"

"I don't think the culprit is anyone working here - they are all hardworking, and honest people," said Ramu. "Could the gems have fallen down and got lost in the grass?"

"I don't think so," said Raj. "The ground in the tent was covered with tarpaulin. They would have noticed if anything had fallen down."

A bird chirped in the branches above. Ramu looked up, making sure he was not sitting directly under it. He had heard that the emperor wanted peacocks, songbirds and other exotic birds in the garden when it was completed.

"Wait, how about birds?" Ramu asked. "My grandma used to say that crows like bright, shiny objects. They are known to take eye-catching items and hide them in their nests. There are so many birds in this garden - could one of them be the culprit?"

Just then, Ramu's mother called out to him.

"I have to go back to work," he said sadly, "but we can meet again during my lunch break if you like."

"Let's do that! Until then, Sid and I will stake out the tent. Let's see if your hunch about the birds is true," said Raj.

Sid and Raj scouted the area around the tent. They found a quiet spot under a tree facing the opening of the tent and settled down. Sid scanned the surrounding area but did not see anything suspicious. People were busy working, some with the help of animals, others in smaller groups. The only people working by themselves were working on calligraphy or carving in marble.

"Let's play a game to pass time while we wait," suggested Raj. "Do you want to play Name-Place-Animal-Thing?"

"I haven't played that game before. How do you play it?" asked Sid.

"One person picks an alphabet and the other person has to say a name, a place, an animal and a thing that begins with that letter," explained Raj. "We take turns playing. You pick a letter, and I can go first to show you."

"How about the letter D?" Sid asked.

"Easy - David, Delhi, Dog, Drum", Raj rattled off. "Your turn, and I select the letter M."

Sid thought for a few seconds. "Name -

Mumtaz; Place - Mexico; Animal....," he paused. "Monkey!"

"Good - what about a 'thing' starting with M?" prodded Raj.

"No, look!" Sid exclaimed, pointing to the tree above the inlay tent. "See that monkey hanging from the tree branch? I saw something shiny in its hands!"

They were onto something!

They quietly followed the monkey as it swung from that tree to the next, and then another. It settled in a tree fork and looked around furtively. When it thought no one was looking, it opened its clenched paw and admired its booty - a bright red jewel! A few minutes later, the monkey carefully put the red stone in a tree hollow.

"Now we know who has been stealing the gems!" exclaimed Raj. "Let's tell Ramu."

CHAPTER THIRTEEN
The Reward

Sid and Raj ran to the nearby area where Ramu was working.

"Ramu, you were right. Only, it wasn't a bird stealing those gems like you thought. It was a monkey, and it hid the gem in that tree hollow," Raj said, pointing at the tree. "You should go tell the supervising architect."

"You both found the culprit - you should tell him," said Ramu.

"If it wasn't for your idea, we wouldn't have looked up in the trees for potential culprits," explained Sid. "Besides, we're both not supposed to be here today. We don't want to draw attention to ourselves."

Ramu told his mother of the discovery and asked her permission to inform Puruji.

"Go ahead *beta,* I'll come along in a few seconds," she said.

Ramu went toward the tomb looking for the site architect.

His mother, Raj, and Sid followed a few steps behind.

"I think we found the culprit," Ramu told Puruji, explaining what the monkey had done. The supervising architect rounded up a few workers and followed Ramu to the tree. The monkey was still sitting in the tree. The workers tried to get the monkey to move by throwing small pebbles near it. The monkey retreated to a higher branch on the tree but kept watch.

One worker climbed up a ladder and cautiously peeped inside the tree hollow. He slowly put his hand inside. He pulled his hand out and displayed a collection of red, green and yellow gems!

Puruji patted Ramu on the back. "Good job, *beta!* That was quick - the emperor is still here. Let me give him the news. Come with me."

They followed Puruji back to the royal procession. Puruji spoke with the emperor and showed him the precious stones. He turned and called Ramu.

Ramu trembled as he bowed before Shah Jahan.

"Puruji informed me that you found the missing jewels. What is your name?" the emperor asked.

"My name is Ramu," he replied. "I work in the garden with my mother. My friends and I found the culprit," he said, pointing to Sid and Raj.

The emperor's advisor called Sid and Raj. They bowed down, mimicking others they had seen bowing.

"You children are clever detectives. Do you also work here?"

"No, your majesty. We were just visiting,"

replied Raj.

Shah Jahan turned to his advisor. "Pay Ramu's parents the reward I promised. Also see to it that Ramu does not have to work for a living, but can attend school instead."

"And for you two," he turned to Sid and Raj. "Pick a memento of your visit today," he said, pointing to a tray.

The tray held miniature replicas of decorative elements of the Taj: flowers carved in marble, mosaic inlaid designs, and marble engraved with flowing calligraphy.

Raj picked up a tiny rose delicately carved in marble. Sid chose a mosaic with multi-colored flowers, admired it, and slipped it into his pocket. They thanked the emperor and went to join Ramu.

"Ramu, you don't have to work here, you can start going to school!" Raj said excitedly.

"Unless I follow your example, and play truant," Ramu quipped.

The trio chose a secluded spot to play a game of freeze tag.

Ramu got tagged and had to stand frozen in his spot while Sid chased Raj.

Suddenly, Raj yelled, "SID! The monkey thief has his hand in your bag!"

Sid stopped in his tracks. He had left his bag unguarded when they had started playing. He raced toward the bag, with Raj close on his heels. The monkey had the camera in its hands. When it saw them, it dropped the camera and scampered away. The camera was turned on, facing them with the lens extended.

"Sid! Hurry!!" shouted Raj. "The camera will click a picture anytime now. We can't be left behind in history!"

"I hope we go back to the 21st century again," Sid wished, as he picked up the camera. It made a high-pitched whirring sound, followed by a bright flash of light that momentarily blinded them.

CHAPTER FOURTEEN
Today Again

Sid blinked a few times, trying to get his vision back. He could see bright spots dancing in front of his eyes, but they reduced with each blink. After a few seconds, he saw a blurry Raj also blinking.

Sid and Raj were back in their own clothes again. Sid turned to look at the Taj. It had no scaffolding, no workers, just tourists. A lot of them. And no monkey. The sun glistened off the white dome behind them.

They were in the same place and time as they were before their little adventure!

'Did all that really happen?' Sid wondered. His heart skipped a beat as he suddenly realized that he did not have his bag.

"My bag!" exclaimed Sid, looking around frantically.

"I have it. I picked it up just when you grabbed the camera. Here you go..." Raj said, handing it over to Sid.

"Great timing! But we didn't get to say goodbye to Ramu," said Sid. "I'm glad that he got a chance to go to school like a normal kid. After all, it was his suspicion that helped us solve the mystery of the missing gems."

"It's sad that many of those precious stones were stolen during the British rule of India," added Raj.

"I read that too," agreed Sid. He looked closely at the camera dial, which was still set to the mode that looked like a clock. "It has to be something with this setting," he thought out loud.

He changed the dial to Auto Mode and

gingerly clicked the button. He shut his eyes and waited. He slowly opened one eye after he heard the shutter click. He was relieved to see the display showing a normal picture, and that nothing had changed around them!

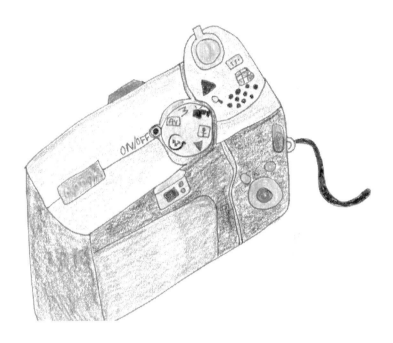

"We're still in the present," said Raj, breathing a sigh of relief. "It must be that time clock mode on the camera dial. That, and you wishing to go back in time. You were right - that is a magical camera!"

"I'll have to safeguard this camera", said

Sid. "I can't even tell anyone else about it. No one will believe me!"

"Let's just not tell anyone," said Raj. "It'll be our little secret!"

"Our little secret," said Sid. He turned off the camera and put it away in his drawstring bag. "Enough pictures for today!"

"I am famished - are you hungry?" asked Raj.

"I feel like I haven't eaten in 350 years!" joked Sid. "These snack bars should help until we reach the car."

"I'll ask our car driver to take us somewhere nice for a late lunch," Raj promised.

When their driver dropped them back at the hotel that evening, their dads were already waiting for them.

"You two look tired," said Mr. Verma. "I hope you both had a more exciting time than we did in office!"

"We did. Raj and I received a wonderful

history lesson at the Taj," said Sid, winking at Raj. His fingers felt the smooth edges of marble in his pocket.

"Oh, I almost forgot. My camera broke this morning," Sid confessed to his dad. "But Raj took me to a bazaar and I got a great deal on an old camera."

"It works better than we expected," smiled Raj. "Don't forget to email the pictures to me, Sid."

"Apart from the camera, did you get any souvenirs of your visit to the Taj?" asked Mr. Cooper.

"We did," answered Raj, pulling out his carved marble rose. "We got some timeless souvenirs from our trip."

"Wow, Raj! That looks so authentic," Raj's dad said, admiring the marble rose. "I've bought souvenirs many times from near the Taj Mahal, but I've never seen anything like this!"

Sid showed off his colorful mosaic inlaid in marble.

"Those are both beautiful," Mr. Cooper said. "We should get a few more to give family and friends."

"We can buy more when we visit the Taj, but I am not parting with this one," said Sid, clutching his memento.

"Don't worry Sid - that one is all yours. So, when will you show me around the Taj?" his dad asked.

"At sunrise on your day off," replied Sid. "I read that the Taj Mahal looks as if it is changing colors during the day. But it looks its best at sunrise and sunset."

"If I can get you out of bed that early," his dad joked.

"One more thing - I think my camera needs a rest, so can we use your camera instead?" Sid requested his dad. "I'm sure we won't have an adventure trying to get pictures with it!"

Raj gave Sid a knowing glance and both boys grinned.

Timeline of the Taj Mahal

1612: Shah Jahan marries Arjumand Banu Begum

1627: Shah Jahan ascends the throne as the fifth Mughal emperor. He gives his wife the title Mumtaz Mahal (Chosen one of the Palace)

1631: Mumtaz dies giving birth to their 14th child

1632: Work begins on a mausoleum for Mumtaz Mahal

1653: Construction of the Taj Mahal complex is completed

1658: Emperor Shah Jahan is overthrown and jailed by his son Aurangzeb

1666: Shah Jahan dies, and is buried alongside Mumtaz Mahal

1908: Lord Curzon, Viceroy of India completes restoration work of the Taj Mahal complex

1914: Indian poet Rabindranath Tagore writes a poem calling the Taj Mahal "a teardrop on the cheek of time"

1983: Taj designated as a UNESCO World Heritage Site

1998: Supreme Court of India orders anti-pollution measures and conservation works to protect Taj Mahal from deterioration

2007: The Taj Mahal is declared one of the winners of the New 7 Wonders of the World

Pictures

A close up of the Taj Mahal as seen from the base

Delicate carvings & inlay designs decorate the walls

The Taj from the great gate

The view of the Taj Mahal from the Red Fort

See pictures from Sid's view at:
http://mysteriesinhistory.org/pix

About The Taj Mahal

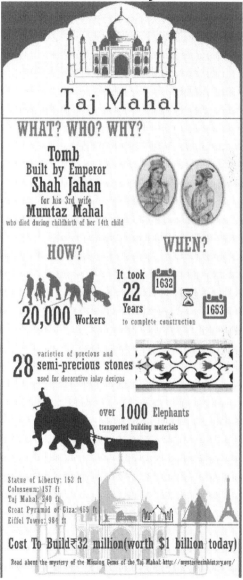

Taj Mahal

WHAT? WHO? WHY?

Tomb
Built by Emperor
Shah Jahan
for his 3rd wife
Mumtaz Mahal
who died during childbirth of her 14th child

HOW?

20,000 Workers

WHEN?

It took
22 Years
to complete construction

1632 — 1653

28 varieties of precious and
semi-precious stones
used for decorative inlay designs

over **1000** Elephants
transported building materials

Statue of Liberty: 152 ft
Colosseum: 157 ft
Taj Mahal: 240 ft
Great Pyramid of Giza: 465 ft
Eiffel Tower: 984 ft

Cost To Build ₹32 million(worth $1 billion today)

Read about the mystery of the Missing Gems of the Taj Mahal: http://mysteriesinhistory.org/

Author

Lyndon is a writer who has been publishing non-fiction internationally since he was in college. He lives in Robbinsville, NJ, loves travel and sightseeing, often dragging his wife and two sons along. He first visited the Taj Mahal at the age of 3, but was inspired to write *Missing Gems of the Taj Mahal* after taking his mystery-book-loving sons to visit the monument in 2015.

Lyndon has more LEGO minifigures than his sons' collections combined. His LEGO lookalike (LegoGuy) was featured in a daily photo series for a year in cities across America and India (http://cerejo.com/legoguy/).

Did you find a picture with a minifigure somewhere in the book?

Hint: It was in one of the pictures at the start of a chapter.

Illustrator

Eleven year old Ananya Chopra is a Jersey girl who loves to draw, paint, and illustrate. Her other hobbies include playing the drums, reading, and playing table tennis. Her dream is to be an artist and also win an Olympic medal in table tennis for USA.

Ananya created all the illustrations for this book between her fifth grade assignments, quizzes, tests and her regular extracurricular activities.

Made in the USA
Las Vegas, NV
18 November 2020